GEORGE to the Rescue!

by Becky Cheston
illustrated by Marsha Solomowitz

Harcourt
SCHOOL PUBLISHERS

Printed in China

ISBN 10: 0-15-351043-9
ISBN 13: 978-0-15-351043-4

Ordering Options
ISBN 10: 0-15-350602-4 (Grade 5 On-Level Collection)
ISBN 13: 978-0-15-350602-4 (Grade 5 On-Level Collection)
ISBN 10: 0-15-357968-4 (package of 5)
ISBN 13: 978-0-15-357968-4 (package of 5)

4 5 6 7 8 9 10   0940   12 11 10 09

George lifted one eyelid to see whether the coast was clear. Two other dogs lay napping near him on the porch. Closest was his best friend, Gwyneth, a light-colored golden retriever. Over by the steps was Dylan, a squat little corgi with an equally squat little tail. The other dogs were guests, here for a week of agility training. They were either resting in the pen or milling around by the hoops and hurdles.

George rose quietly and tiptoed down the steps. Quickly, he made his way into the woods near the barn. George hated that he had to sneak off in order to spend time with his friend Woody. However, George was an English springer spaniel— a *sporting* dog—and he couldn't let any of the other dogs know that he liked to play with—

"Hey, Georgie!" called a squirrel from high in a tree.

George looked up. There was his friend Woody, crisscrossing down the branches of the big oak tree. He looked gleeful as he leaped to the ground, landing in front of George.

"Hi, Woody!" George said.

Woody spotted an acorn, picked it up, and nibbled it. "Where have you been?"

George hung his head. It was true—he hadn't been back in these woods for days. Things had been busy this week at Mirabelli Farms. On Monday, the summer's first agility session had begun. A total of ten dogs—besides George, Gwyneth, and Dylan—were now housed on the grounds. The dogs would be trained to jump through hoops, slither under boards, and race around barrels. Some might eventually even compete in agility contests.

The old horse barn, converted to a guest house, was noisy with trainers, dog owners, and their kids. The old riding corral, set up with tunnels, hurdles, and hoops, bustled with activity. George and Gwyneth also took part. Dylan, a herding dog who was not exactly built for agility, was free to prowl the grounds.

"It's been really hard to get away this week." George watched Woody rummage in the earth, pull out a second nut, and attack it with gusto. "Hey, Woody, you act like you haven't eaten in weeks."

"Food's been scarce lately," Woody explained.

"Really?" George was surprised because he knew that Woody and his family and friends always kept stashes of food.

Woody said, "Lately, there's been—"

All of a sudden, the woods echoed with screams. Overhead, squirrels bounded through the trees, erupting with turbulent chatter. One of them scrambled down Woody's oak, stopping on the trunk when he saw George.

"Don't panic, Filbert," said Woody. "It's only our friend George."

"It's happened again," Filbert said. "The food we gathered this morning? It's gone."

George listened as the two squirrels explained. During the past week, their precious stores of food had been disappearing. Guards had been posted to keep watch over the food, but they proved no match for the scavenging raccoons. When George asked to hear more, a loud whistle pierced the air. He turned to see ten-year-old Nina Mirabelli running toward him.

"I've got to go!" George turned back to the squirrels, but they had already vanished.

George returned to the riding corral with Nina and trained with the other dogs in the corral. After the day's training ended, George followed Nina around, begging for treats.

Gwyneth fell in step beside George. "Want to go hang out by the barn?" she asked. "Pepper's over there." Pepper, who often trained at Mirabelli Farms, was a sleek greyhound.

"I guess," said George. What he really wanted to do was help Woody stop the thieving raccoons. George could hardly sneak off to the woods now, though, with all the dogs around. He followed Gwyneth to the shady side of the barn, where four or five dogs were resting.

"Hey, you two!" called out a Labrador retriever named Reggie. "Tell the Mirabellis to be a little more generous with the biscuits next time, okay?"

"Next time get there sooner instead of following Maggie around everywhere," Gwyneth said. Maggie was an energetic border collie who always seemed to be in motion. At the moment, in fact, she was feeling giddy, happily running in circles.

George and Gwyneth sat down with the other dogs for a nap. When it appeared that the other dogs were dozing, George carefully tried to tiptoe back to the woods.

"Where are you off to?" Gwyneth asked.

"Uh, nowhere," George stuttered.

"Come on, George. Do you think I haven't noticed your little excursions into the woods? What's going on?" Gwyneth demanded.

By now the other dogs had woken up and taken an interest. George sighed and confessed about his friendship with Woody the squirrel.

Reggie laughed. "That's your big secret? I've got lots of squirrel friends back home, too."

"There's no shame in befriending other animals," Pepper said. "I'm good friends with a cricket and a pigeon, you know."

Even Gwyneth seemed to understand, much to George's relief. Since his friends didn't have anything against squirrels, he decided to tell them about Woody's problem. Maybe they could help.

Later George led his fellow dogs to Woody's tree. George stopped and called to his squirrel friend. Tentatively, Woody made his way down the tree. George convinced him that his dog friends were willing to help Woody and the other squirrels. Delighted, Woody called over some of his squirrel friends. Then they brainstormed what could be done to fend off those raccoons. Soon the animals had cooked up a plan.

The dogs paired off and went to hide near the trees that held the most sizable stores of food. George stood guard with Gwyneth near Woody's tree. Above, the squirrel neighborhood was settling down for the night. The light grew dim as the first pink streaks of sunset appeared in the sky.

"It looks like we may have to come back tomorrow," Gwyneth said, worried.

George had hit the pinnacle of excitement just thinking about helping his friends. Now he felt the letdown of disappointment. He was a bright, puffy balloon, deflating with a slow hiss. Soon the Mirabellis would come looking for them. Though he expected to hear Nina's voice calling them all home, he heard Pepper bark instead.

"This way!" shouted Gwyneth. She ran in the direction of Filbert's tree, George at her heels. Now they could hear all the other dogs barking. When they arrived, Pepper and Dylan were on their hind legs, pawing at the tree. Nearby, Reggie and Maggie had two raccoons cornered on the ground.

"How dare you steal from my squirrel friends!" George shouted.

"What's wrong with you raccoons?" said Reggie. "Why don't you get your own food?!"

One of the raccoons was shaking, but the other looked unfazed. Standing on his hind legs, he sneered, "Get our own food? That's not how we do things. Look at you—a bunch of herders and retrievers. There's not a guard dog among you!"

At that remark, the dogs growled fiercely at the raccoons. Just then a third raccoon came waddling clumsily down the tree.

"I had to drop the food," she said. "I can take on squirrels, but sorry—these dogs mean business." Without another word, the raccoons quickly scampered away.

"Uh-oh!" said Gwyneth. "Do you hear that?"

The dogs heard two sharp whistles, then came Nina's voice calling, "Georgie! Gwy-neth!" In a few seconds, they saw Nina and her father making their way into the woods.

Nina spotted them first. "There you are, Georgie! What are you doggies doing out here so late?"

Soon all the dogs had been rounded up, scolded, and hugged. As they followed the Mirabellis back to the farm, George spotted Woody dashing alongside them through the bushes. "Thank you!" he chattered to George. "Please also thank your friends—I mean, *my* new friends!"

Think Critically

1. Why is George afraid to tell his friends about Woody?

2. What happens when George tells the other dogs about his friendship with Woody?

3. At the beginning of the story, did you suspect that Woody had a food problem? Why or why not?

4. Find a phrase that helps you picture how George feels as he realizes that the raccoons might not appear. What do you think of this description?

5. If you could be any character in this story, which one would you be, and why?

 **Social Studies**

Dogs in Other Countries What kinds of dogs are popular in other countries? Use library resources or the Internet to find the answer. Summarize your findings.

School-Home Connection Tell family members about the story. Then talk about some dogs you know and how they are like or different from the dogs in the story.

GRADE 5

Lesson 24

WORD COUNT

1,308

GENRE

Fantasy

LEVEL

See TG or go Online

Go online Harcourt Leveled
Readers Online Database

ISBN-13: 978-0-15-351043-4
ISBN-10: 0-15-351043-9

9 780153 510434

90000 >

Harcourt
SCHOOL PUBLISHERS

A Friendly Field Trip

by Natalie Behar

illustrated by Molly Delaney

Harcourt
SCHOOL PUBLISHERS